# The Bear Ate Your Sandwich

## JULIA SARCONE-ROACH

Alfred A. Knopf 🐎 New York

By now I think you know what happened to your sandwich. But you may not know *how* it happened. So let me tell you.

It all started with the bear.

The morning air was warm and bright when the bear
stepped out of his den. He stretched and sniffed.

The scent of ripe berries drifted toward him and led to a wonderful discovery.

After a berry feast,
the bear curled up
in the sunlight and
listened to the
buzzing of the bees.

Before long, he was asleep.

Once the rumbling stopped, the bear found himself in a new forest.

It was like nothing he'd ever seen before.

This forest had many great
climbing spots.

The trees were still
itchy here.

There was good bark for scratching.

And the mud squished nicely under his feet.

There were many interesting
smells in this forest.

But some of the tastiest ones had already been found.

Leafy green smells led the bear to new fun.

And *that* is when

he

saw

it.

There it was.

Your beautiful and delicious sandwich. All alone.

He waited to make sure no one saw him

(not even the sandwich)

before he made his move.

It was such a great sandwich.
The bear loved it.

But just as he was
almost finished,
he heard

Sniff
Snuffle
Slobber
Snort

behind him.

He had been seen!

The bear was so surprised that he ran—

out of the park

and down the street—

until he spotted a very tall tree.

From the top of the tree, the bear could
see his forest. It was time to go home.

The waves rocked the bear and he began to doze.

When he opened his eyes, he heard the breeze in familiar branches and the birds' and bugs' evening song.

Well, the bear
made it home
just fine.

I saw it all. I tried to save your sandwich. I was able to save this little bit of lettuce here. The bear dropped it as he ran off, but I couldn't save the rest. I'm sorry to have to tell you about your sandwich this way,

## To Adam

"Enjoy every sandwich."
—Warren Zevon

THIS IS A BORZOI BOOK PUBLISHED BY ALFRED A. KNOPF

Copyright © 2015 by Julia Sarcone-Roach

All rights reserved. Published in the United States by Alfred A. Knopf, an imprint of Random House Children's Books, a division of Random House LLC, a Penguin Random House Company, New York. Knopf, Borzoi Books, and the colophon are registered trademarks of Random House LLC.

Visit us on the Web! randomhouse.com/kids

Educators and librarians, for a variety of teaching tools, visit us at RHTeachersLibrarians.com

*Library of Congress Cataloging-in-Publication Data*

Sarcone-Roach, Julia, author, illustrator.

The bear ate your sandwich / by Julia Sarcone-Roach. — First edition.

p.  cm.

Summary: When a sandwich goes missing, it seems that a bear is the likely culprit.

ISBN 978-0-375-85860-4 (trade) — ISBN 978-0-375-95860-1 (lib. bdg.) — ISBN 978-0-307-98242-1 (ebook)

[1. Bears—Fiction. 2. City and town life—Fiction. 3. Sandwiches—Fiction. 4. Dogs—Fiction. 5. Humorous stories.] I. Title.

PZ7.S242Be 2015

[E]—dc23

2014013199

The illustrations in this book were created using acrylic paint and pencil.

MANUFACTURED IN CHINA

January 2015   10 9 8 7 6   First Edition